PRESERVATION DENTAL

• 371 E Main St - Northville 48167 •

Where Do Baby Teeth Go?

By...

Denise Mrakitsch Jenkins

Illustrations by...

Walter Jenkins

First Page Publications

12103 Merriman • Livonia • MI • 48150
1-800-343-3034 • Fax 734-525-4420
www.firstpagepublications.com

Library of Congress Cataloging-in-Publication Data

Jenkins, Denise Mrakitsch.
     Where do baby teeth go? / by Denise Mrakitsch Jenkins;
illustrations by Walter Jenkins
     p. cm.
     SUMMARY: When Lily loses her first tooth, her parents
tell her about the Tooth Fairy, the dentist, and proper
dental care. She and her brother meet Betsy Floss, Mr.
2th DK, and the Sugar Bugs.
     ISBN 1-928623-37-9

     1. Teeth--Juvenile fiction. [1. Teeth--Fiction.]
I. Jenkins, Walter. II. Title.

PZ7.J41335Whe 2004   [Fic]
                    QBI04-800013

First Page Publications
12103 Merriman
Livonia, MI 48150
www.firstpagepublications.com

I dedicate this storybook
to my son, Brent, as he receives
his Doctor of Dental Surgery
degree from
Dalhousie University.
May 2003

Special thanks to my friend,
Doctor Bill, for his encouragement...
And for allowing me to share his characters
with the readers.
In loving memory of my dad, Pete...
Proud of his grandson's career choice and
happy to have kept three of his very own
teeth with the help of Dr. Bill!

"Mommy, I'm getting tired. I think it's time to go to bed."
Lily's Mom looked surprised. "My, my, little missy, I don't think I've ever heard you say that!"

Daddy was playing a game with Lily's little brother. "I'll bet it has something to do with that tooth that fell out after dinner." Andy looked at his dad and asked, "What's the big deal?"

Lily rolled her eyes and said, "You are such a baby. Don't you know that when your baby teeth fall out you put them under your pillow and the Tooth Fairy brings you a surprise when you are sleeping?" Andy started to wiggle his front tooth. Lily made a face at him. "Your teeth aren't ready yet, silly Andy, 'cause you're still a baby. But me, I am six-and-a-half years old!" Lily reached over to give her dad a kiss on her way up to bed.

"Sweet dreams, Lily. Brush the rest of those teeth, otherwise the Tooth Fairy might fly right by."

Lily was already on her way up the stairs. "Okay, Daddy."

Lily washed her face and hands and brushed her teeth. As Mommy tucked her in, Lily tucked her tooth, the very first to fall out, under her pillow.

It was carefully wrapped in a tissue. She stuffed the tissue in a little satin envelope Auntie Cece had given to her for this very special occasion. "I hope the Tooth Fairy can find my tooth. Mommy, what if it falls under the bed while I'm sleeping?" Mommy said it would be fine and gave her a kiss on the forehead before turning out the light. Lily fell fast asleep with her thoughts in search of the Tooth Fairy house.

3

4

The next morning Andy was already up and eating a bowl of cereal when Lily came running into the kitchen. "Look! Look! The Tooth Fairy brought me a shiny coin! And an itty bitty note with sparkles all over! She flew in my window and there's gold dust on my window sill." Andy jumped up to see the coin and the note.

Daddy gave Lily a big hug and read the note aloud, "Here's a shiny coin for a sparkling clean tooth! Keep up the good work." He smiled at her, "Lily, I am so proud of you. You must brush your teeth extra well."

Lily nodded her head, "I do Daddy. I brush after every meal and I don't eat as much candy as Andy does!"

5

Andy put his head down. Daddy saw how sad he was. "Andy, it's okay, one day you will lose a tooth and the Tooth Fairy will bring you a surprise too."

"Mommy, is there candy in my cereal?" Andy was holding up his spoon looking at a little marshmallow.

"No, honey, it's not candy. But there is a lot of sugar in it. Make sure you brush after breakfast to clean away all the little sugar bugs."

Andy's eyes got real big. "Sugar bugs? What are they?"

Daddy said, "Well, son, there's sugar in a lot of the foods we eat. Sometimes the sugar sticks to our teeth. You want to brush to clean away the sugar — or the sugar bugs — as Mommy calls them."

Lily reached for the box of cereal. Andy was quick to remind Lily that she liked the same cereal he did. "See Lily you eat the same as me. So you've got sugar bugs too." She wiggled her nose, and then ignored him.

Mommy was sitting in the dining room when the phone rang. "Hello." There was a little pause. "Oh yes, we'll be there. And I think Lily has something to show Doctor Ford. See you tomorrow."

"That was the dentist's office," Mommy said. "We have appointments tomorrow to get our teeth cleaned and checked."

Andy asked, "Me too?"

"Of course," Mommy said. Andy looked past Lily and smiled at his dad. Daddy winked back at him.

"Don't forget, tonight we are going to Grandma and Grandpa's house for dinner," he said. Lily got all excited.

"Can we see the Tooth Fairy house?"

"Where's the Tooth Fairy house?" Andy asked.

Mommy said, "Well, it's on our way home from Grandma and Grandpa's house. Sometimes you are too sleepy to stay awake and see it."

Andy put his bowl in the sink and started to walk away. "I'm not going to fall asleep tonight. Right now I'm going to brush my teeth." And off he went.

"Hi, Grandma, look!" Lily ran up to the front porch and smiled so wide that Grandma laughed. "Oh my, just when did that happen? Let's go find my camera to take your picture." Lily went off with Grandma, talking about the missing tooth and the visit from the Tooth Fairy.

Andy came along with Mommy and Daddy. He was looking sad because now Grandma was making a big fuss over that silly missing tooth. "Do I have to be six years old before I lose my baby teeth?" "No" Mommy said. "Everyone is different. You can ask Dr. Ford about that tomorrow. Okay?" Andy smiled and nodded his head. Daddy took Andy's hand and followed the girls into the kitchen. "Something smells good," Daddy said.

"I made your favorite oatmeal cookies," Grandma said as she pulled a tray from the oven. Andy looked over Grandma's shoulder and asked, "Do they have sugar bugs in them?" Grandma almost dropped the pan. "There are no bugs in these cookies. Those are raisins." Mommy and Daddy laughed. Lily told Grandma the story about the sugar bugs that get on your teeth and how to brush them away.

"What's all this talk about bugs?" Grandpa had just woken up from a nap. Andy raced over to give him a hug and tell him all about the sugar bugs. "Well, I wish someone had told me about those sugar bugs a long time ago. Maybe then I wouldn't have these false teeth!" Grandpa said. "What are false teeth?" Lily asked. Grandpa explained that he hadn't taken good care of his permanent teeth when he was younger and how the dentist tried to help him but he didn't listen. Now he had false teeth.

Andy asked what *per man ent* teeth were. Lily quickly jumped in to say, "That's what I'm going to get now where the baby tooth fell out." Grandpa gave them both a big hug and said, "You are very lucky your mom and dad take good care of their teeth and they make sure you do too. I hope you'll never need to get false teeth. Let's keep our fingers crossed." He crossed his fingers and helped Andy cross his. Lily could do it all by herself. Mommy and Daddy crossed their fingers too.

After dinner it was time to head for home.
As they drove away they waved goodbye and
Grandma called out to them, "Don't forget to look
for the Tooth Fairy house!" They were driving for
a long time. It was getting dark outside. The sky
was full of stars and the moon was very bright.
Lily and Andy were getting sleepy. Lily asked,
"Are we almost there?" "Where?" Daddy asked.
Although he could barely keep his eyes open,
Andy said quietly, "The Tooth Fairy house."
Mommy and Daddy both looked around.
"Pretty soon," Mommy said. After a couple
more minutes Lily and Andy were both
nodding off when all of a sudden Mommy said
softly, "There it is." Lily rubbed her eyes and
Andy opened his lids just long enough to see
the gold dome in the sky.

It was beautiful. For a moment Daddy slowed down and said, "See it up there?" Two little voices in the back seat said, "Yes, Daddy."

Lily said, "It's so shiny." Mommy said, "When the Tooth Fairy collects all the baby teeth she checks them over. If they are clean and bright they go in the golden dome of her castle." Andy wearily asked, "What if they have sugar bugs?" Mommy answered, "Then she tosses them out in the night sky." "I'm always going to keep my teeth clean," Lily said just before a big yawn. As Andy nodded off to sleep he uttered, "Me too, Lily." Lily reached over to hold her little brother's hand. Soon they were both sound asleep.

The next day the whole family got ready to go to the dentist. Daddy was looking in the mirror and pulling some kind of thread through his teeth. "What's that Daddy?" Andy asked. "It's called dental floss and it cleans between your teeth. Did you brush your teeth already?" "Not yet," Andy said and went looking for Lily. She was putting her little note and the shiny coin in her little pouch.

"What are you doing, Lily?" Andy asked. Lily didn't even look at him as she answered, "I'm going to show Dr. Ford what I got from the Tooth Fairy." Andy went looking for his mother.

Mommy was brushing her teeth. Andy reached for his brush. "Mommy, do I brush my teeth good?" She nodded yes. "When will I lose my baby teeth?" he asked again. She shrugged her shoulders and continued to brush. "You brush good too, Mommy," Andy said. "I'm going to tell Dr. Ford." When she was all through she gave him a hug and a kiss on the cheek. "Keep up the good work!" Andy kept brushing and thought, *Hmm, that's what the Tooth Fairy note said.*

At Dr. Ford's office there were books and puzzles and a really nice lady at the front desk. She knew everyone's name when they came in. Lily's friend from school, Emily, was sitting in the lobby. "Hi, Emily, guess what?" Lily ran over to show off the missing tooth.

The nice lady at the desk said, "Hi Andy. Do you want to go first?" He was so excited that she knew his name. He raced past Lily. Pretty soon he was sitting in this great big chair with lots of cool stuff around him.

When Dr. Ford came in Andy told him about the sugar bugs and asked when his baby teeth would fall out and on and on he went. Finally Dr. Ford said, "Whoa, partner. Give me a chance to answer. First of all, let me take a look in your mouth. Everyone loses baby teeth at different times. You could lose one today or tomorrow…" Andy smiled even though the dentist

I'm going to be a dentist when I grow up!

was looking in his mouth, "…or maybe not any until you are six or seven." Andy scowled. Dr Ford said, "Why do you ask?" "Lily lost a tooth and she got a shiny coin from the Tooth Fairy." Dr. Ford smiled. "Well, your teeth look pretty shiny, and when they start to fall out, I bet you'll get a shiny coin too."

Andy looked a little scared. "They're not ALL going to fall out like my Grandpa's, are they? He's got false teeth." Dr. Ford smiled and spoke softly, "Oh no. But you always have to take good care of your teeth. After all, you need them to eat and to talk and they make you smile!" Dr. Ford stepped on something under the chair and it went up and then down. Andy thought this was a pretty cool place. When the dentist was all finished checking his teeth he gave Andy a new toothbrush and his very own dental floss.

"After I see your mom and your dad and Lily we can talk about those sugar bugs. Okay? Why don't you ask Lily to come in next?" Dr. Ford made Andy feel very special.

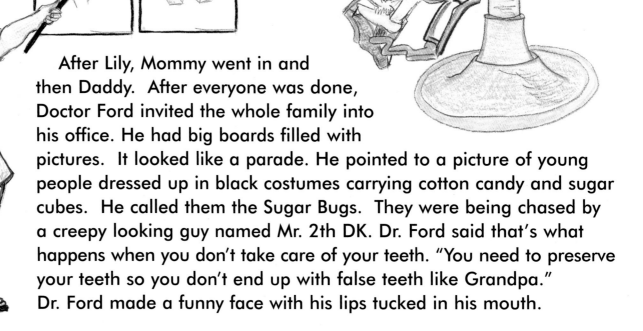

After Lily, Mommy went in and then Daddy. After everyone was done, Doctor Ford invited the whole family into his office. He had big boards filled with pictures. It looked like a parade. He pointed to a picture of young people dressed up in black costumes carrying cotton candy and sugar cubes. He called them the Sugar Bugs. They were being chased by a creepy looking guy named Mr. 2th DK. Dr. Ford said that's what happens when you don't take care of your teeth. "You need to preserve your teeth so you don't end up with false teeth like Grandpa." Dr. Ford made a funny face with his lips tucked in his mouth.

There was a sweet looking lady that Dr. Ford called Betsy Floss. Mommy laughed. Dr. Ford showed everyone how to use the floss he gave them to clean in between their teeth. He said to do it whenever they could.

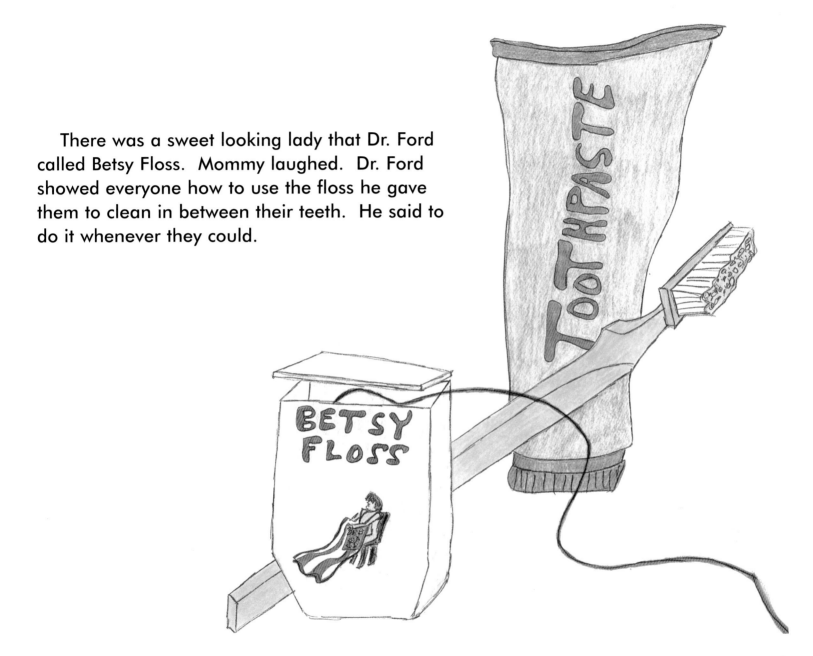

Finally, there was a beautiful picture of the Tooth Fairy. Lily asked if her friend Emily could come in to look at the picture because she didn't believe Lily when she told her about the gold dust on the window sill or that she had seen the Tooth Fairy house. Doctor Ford said it was okay for Emily to come in and he winked at Daddy. Emily saw the Tooth Fairy with her very own eyes. "But where's the Tooth Fairy house?" she asked. Dr. Ford raised his eyebrows and looked at Daddy. Daddy looked at Mommy.

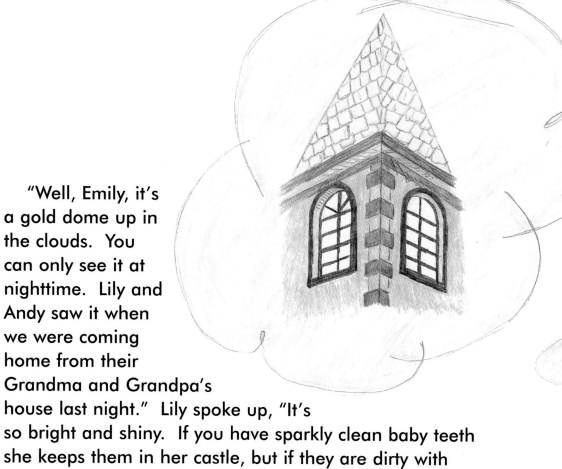

"Well, Emily, it's
a gold dome up in
the clouds. You
can only see it at
nighttime. Lily and
Andy saw it when
we were coming
home from their
Grandma and Grandpa's
house last night." Lily spoke up, "It's
so bright and shiny. If you have sparkly clean baby teeth
she keeps them in her castle, but if they are dirty with
sugar bugs they are tossed aside."

Dr. Ford looked at Mommy and smiled, "Were you on the highway when you saw the Tooth Fairy house?" "Yes," Mommy said.

Daddy added, "The city skyline is full of magic."

Dr. Ford agreed.

The End